CAPTAIN MARVEL

MEET THE MARVELS

By Nadia Shammas
Illustrated by Shane Clester

Published by Scholastic Australia in 2023.

Scholastic Australia Pty Limited
PO Box 579 Gosford NSW 2250
ABN 11 000 614 577
www.scholastic.com.au

Part of the Scholastic Group
Sydney • Auckland • New York • Toronto • London • Mexico City • New Delhi • Hong Kong • Buenos Aires • Puerto Rico

ISBN 978-1-76152-057-0

Printed in China.

Scholastic Australia's policy, in association with its printers, is to use papers that are renewable and made efficiently from wood grown in responsibly managed forests, so as to minimise its environmental footprint.

ALERT!!
JERSEY CITY
IN TROUBLE!

One day, Carol Danvers was helping Kamala Khan with her training. They were also known as the Super Heroes Captain Marvel and Ms. Marvel!

Ms. Marvel had named herself after Captain Marvel, so she was excited to learn from her hero.

Suddenly, their training was interrupted by an alarm.

'A distress call!' exclaimed Captain Marvel. 'Looks like training is over for now. The city needs our help!'

Flying to the scene, Ms. Marvel and Captain Marvel were shocked to find a giant alien plant **destroying the city!**

'I've never seen anything like it,' said Ms. Marvel.

'We have to stop it, or it's going to tear downtown apart!' said Captain Marvel, springing to action.

Captain Marvel and Ms. Marvel did their best to stop the mysterious giant plant. Captain Marvel sliced through vines with her energy blasts, and Ms. Marvel used her embiggening powers to make her hands larger so she could carry people to safety.

Then Ms. Marvel noticed that the vines weren't trying to grab people or harm them.

'The plant seems to be looking for something,' she called to Captain Marvel. 'Should we try to talk to it?'

But Captain Marvel kept fighting.

The plant's vines began to grow back, angrier than before! The plant **grabbed** Captain Marvel and retreated with her under the streets!

'What am I going to do now?' cried Ms. Marvel.

'If I want to get Captain Marvel back, I'm going to need some help!'

There was only one person to call: Captain Marvel's good friend **Monica Rambeau!**

Monica Rambeau was also the Super Hero called Spectrum. Spectrum had the power to turn herself into any form of light or energy.

Spectrum and Ms. Marvel decided to follow the plant underground, where they quickly found other vines. The vines seemed similar to the ones that had attacked the city, but they weren't quite the same.

'They look like they're sick,' Spectrum commented.

Ms. Marvel and Spectrum followed the vines out to the reservoir at the edge of the city, where they found the roots and then the core of the plant.

'Look—there she is!' Ms. Marvel exclaimed, pointing to the trapped Captain Marvel.

'This plant pod looks alien in nature,' Spectrum said. 'It must have fallen to Earth by accident and got washed down a storm drain.'

The vines appeared to be dormant. Ms. Marvel tried to be very, very careful, but the moment she touched Captain Marvel, the vines **sprang back to life!**

Ms. Marvel gulped. 'Uh-oh,' she said.

Before Spectrum could blast the plant with her energy beams, Ms. Marvel stepped in front of her.

'Wait! Captain Marvel did the same thing and got caught—and there were even more vines then!' Ms. Marvel cried. 'There has to be another way.'

But no matter how hard Ms. Marvel and Spectrum tried to fight off the vines, the plant surrounded them!

'Instead of fighting, let's try to communicate with it,' said Ms. Marvel.

'How can we do that?' asked Spectrum.

'You could turn into light,' suggested Ms. Marvel. 'Plants respond to light!'

Spectrum began to use her powers to turn into light. 'It's working!' she said.'I can understand it!'

Finally happy to be understood, the plant stopped attacking. Ms. Marvel quickly ran to Captain Marvel, who began to wake up!

'Ms. Marvel, you had it right. This plant wasn't trying to hurt anyone at all!' said Spectrum. 'It was trying to communicate!

This poor plant fell from space, and it's been searching for the kind of soil, water and light that it needs, which can't be found on Earth. It was just scared and wanted to go home,' said Spectrum.

'I'm really proud of you, Ms. Marvel,' said Captain Marvel. 'I didn't listen when you tried to explain, but you found a way to save the day. I guess you're the one who trained me today!'

Beaming with joy, Ms. Marvel said to Captain Marvel and Spectrum, 'You both inspire me so much! Thanks for being the best mentors ever!'

'Now we have to help this plant!' said Ms. Marvel.

'I have just the thing at home,' said Captain Marvel. 'It's a device that will tell us exactly which planet this plant came from by the soil still found on its roots! Now there's only one mystery left.'